TEENAGE GRAVE II

Copyright © 2023 by the individual authors
Designed by Ira Rat

This is a work of fiction. Names, characters, businesses, places, events, locales, and incidents are either the products of the author's imagination or used in a fictitious manner. Any resemblance to actual persons, living or dead, or actual events is purely coincidental.

This book may not be reproduced in whole or in part, except for the inclusion of brief quotations in a review, without permission in writing from the author or publisher. No part of this publication may be reproduced, stored in or introduced into retrieval system, or transmitted, in any form, or by any means (electronic, mechanical, photocopying, recording, or otherwise), without prior permission of the publisher.

Requests for permission should be directed to
filthylootpress@gmail.com

THE NEST WITHIN **RICHARD** 05
LEAD THE BLIND **LUTZ** 25
MISBEGOTTEN **VIDTO** 53
FOUND FAMILY **QUENELL** 91

filthyloot.com

THE NEST WITHIN
SAM RICHARD

She writhes and contorts slowly, freezing in time on occasion, as if she were glitching out. Maybe the connection is bad, a narrow buffer between the live-stream and the action in front of the camera. All that information sent through a signal in the air, then hardwired down into the depths of the earth, all before coming back up, spitting back into the air, and displayed on the screen in crystal clear quality. Or at least that's how it should have gone.

Instead she clips in and out of movement. Sometimes repeating back minute action she'd already taken. Like watching a chameleon walk across a branch. Slow. Reverse imitating the trajectory of their limbs. Alive, but almost unalive. Like a character in a dying arcade game.

She's alive. Not unalive at all. Shimmering sweaty skin on the other side of the world, or just the other side of the block. No way of knowing. Her moans real; or real enough to get the job done. Human at the very least.

Her self-exposure, somehow more intimate than seems normal. Not just seeing her body, not just seeing those parts generally kept between lovers, but seeming to bare an essential portion of herself in the act. In this act. Whatever it actually is.

She moves up and down on the toy, vigorously. Animalistically. In that way that makes you breathe heavily even though you want to remain cool, composed. In a way that makes you see stars and heightens the sensation of your heart pounding in your chest.

The blood swells.

It's never like this. Not with the separation of a screen, of the tangled wires below. This is what it's like with someone real. With someone here, in the room. And it almost feels like it. Like she's in here, breathing heavily with you–into you. Her warmth and strength and grace and pure eroticism funneling not just into your eyes, but penetrating your soul.

But she glitches again. She's moving both forward and backward at once, both where her body was and will be all existing at the same time. You don't want to miss anything. You don't want to rob yourself of whatever this is, but every single time you get close, every single time you can hear her moans vibrate through your skin, the glitching gets worse.

And worse.

And worse again. Compounded and fractured.

So you reset the wi-fi, hoping it won't take all of 5 minutes to get back to normal. Praying that it's just an issue on your end and not an issue on hers. Or the server. Or the hosting company. Or your provider. Or somewhere, deep in the wires. The blood dissipates while you wait, now less aroused and more anticipatory. More curious.

But could she be on this block? In this city? The state? The country? Would it matter if she lived next door.

But it feels like she knows you, like she's peered deeply into all your fears. Strangely. You know you've only lurked, never typed a word, but when she stares into that camera it's like she's speaking to you. To every part of you. Microcosmically.

Wi-fi is still resetting and you feel like a fool. Like a child. Like the kind of person who expects everything be given to them. The entitlement of another's love. But you swear this is different. This isn't some incel shit. *Right?* It's a connection. A new thing, not weird ass behavior from a nutjob online. Inside, she's calling to you.

The icon flashes a few times and she's back on the screen. Upon refresh nothing has changed, aside from her position, now on her back, long legs in the air, arm at her side, reaching around her hip to push the toy in and out and in and out. The refreshed urgency of arousal runs down your spine. But she's still doing it; moving unnaturally. Like a spider gently plucking at strings on a web to make sure they're taut and pulling back to pluck again. She's shifting. Phasing almost, but still here.

Still crawling into you. Into those secret places you have buried deep inside that you never show anyone. That you've never allowed another into. All parts of her stare at you from the screen. She's rooting around in there, re-wiring and bending the circuits.

Her movements flow arrhythmically; her shadows following closely, but not too closely. A blurred line around her that mirrors and drags. She's cutting through the air. She's penetrating everyone watching. It's perfect. Comfortable. Intimate in a new, unknowable way.

Before she climaxes, before you can climax, the feed cuts to black. Your heart drops in your chest, hitting your stomach and sending cold rushing through your veins. Disappointment yes, but also grief, somehow. *Grief?* Yes, grief. Deep sorrowful mourning. You try to shake it off but it's already sunk in. The cursor hangs over the close button, but you notice that the feed hasn't gone silent. Just dark.

Like someone threw something over the camera or turned off the lights.

The wet sound of penetration still pours from the small laptop speakers, barely edging out your own panicked heartbeat in rattling your ears. The sorrow is gone, but apprehension has taken its place. What previously felt like a free-exchange of sexual activity between consenting adults now seems grimy and wrong. Does she know the feed is still live? Is this a part of the performance?

Sitting at the precipice between elation and trepidation gives you goosebumps and a new, and intense, energy crawls across your genitals. Almost primordial in urgency, you go to work on yourself, setting the cadence of your pleasure to the sounds of hers. It doesn't take long before you're spent.

Delirious.

Exhausted.

Content.

Darkness pulls you deeper into your chair and you pass out to her wet sound still radiating around you. It follows you into your dreams.

Wires pulling at you from below. The corpse of a fox in a darkened alley, decaying fluids running out its mouth, into a sewer grate. A soft hand on your thigh; maybe too close, but also comfortable and reassuring. Veins on concrete, shuddering at your touch. An up-close mouth, slurping raw meat off of bones. Being surrounded by cold flesh. Then, darkness.

The birds are cawing outside the window of your cramped single-room apartment when you come to. It's still a little dark out, but the early morning sun is threatening to crest over the horizon line. You clean yourself up in the bathroom and come back to the laptop, awakening it from its sleep. Crust still in your eyes.

The window is still open to the cam-site, but she's gone. Mild slopping noises fill your ears, but they aren't coming from the speakers. It's hot. So hot you're dizzy. Like being way too high.

A quick search on the history bar of your cam account shows nothing. You haven't watched anything all night. Or the day before. You double check that you aren't logged out, but you are so it should be there. Nothing. No viewing history. Maybe they had a server crash. Browser history is the same. Nothing for the past 2 days. *The fuck.*

What was her handle, *Sleaze-something-13*? Nothing comes up. You try everything you can think to fill the 'something' spot. Nothing works. Empty. *The fuck was the 'something?'*

Search and search and search. Frustration and anger and abject terror.

She was real. It was real. A mantra over and over in your mind.

The blood pools.

A pat pat pat sound and dampness on your sweating neck and shoulder. Blood on your hand. It's coming from your ear. The squishing drone gets louder until something pops. But there's no pain. A pressure release. Still just a trickle of blood. The sound is gone. Still the birds outside, singing to the rising sun.

Still the blood.

You clean yourself up again in your grimy bathroom and throw on a pair of not clean but not too dirty pants and a fresh shirt. The room is off. The floor shifts under you, as if it's breathing. Snake-like veins crawl inside the wood across the floor. One underfoot and you yelp. It reacts to your touch. Like arousal.

The door slams behind you as you run from the house.

Fresh air.

Food.

Reality.

The world is suddenly so bright. Crystalline in intensity. Vibrant and horrible smells fill your nose. It's beautiful and awful and you can't stop shaking. Trembling.

The pat pat pat is happening again. Blood collects, staining your shirt. Squicky sounds fill your ears, but at a low level. Nothing pops. You're still so hot. Sweating through your shirt.

Bitter, old coffee and stale donuts are the order of the day, bought at the gas station around the corner.

Cameras are everywhere, watching. Would it feel different if they were just listening? You imagine them covered with a fluid-stained towel. The blood swells.

She dances in your mind, profanely. Beautifully. Your heartbeat increases, walls of your blood vessels hard against the quickly flowing blood. Rigid in all possible ways.

Her sound, no longer in your ears, but off in the distance. The pain of separation, as though you've known anything but in your life. But it isn't just isolation and loneliness, it's a severed response, deep in the lizard brain. Like life was stolen. Love was stolen. Connection and oneness and unification with the fucking universe. Once there and now gone.

In the blink of an eye. The sound fades. Panic sets in.

Why are they all staring? But the street is mostly empty. Someone drives by and they pay no attention to you. But the cameras see. On every building. Ogling. Peering. Surveilling.

Feels like a bad trip, but you haven't had drugs in

years. Outside is fucked, so you go back home. Not satisfied. Not anything but broken.

Back to the computer. Desperate searches on every social media. *She has to have one.* Every search engine. Various configurations of the *something* word with additional search tags. *Model. Sex worker. Cam girl. Alt-model.* Old school message boards you haven't been to since high school that somehow still exist, naming names, sharing and selling images and videos culled from private cam shows and fansites. The bottom end of the trade. Rats and snakes making a buck selling unknowing people's work. Selling unknowing people's bodies and souls to waiting masses of scumbags.

It leaves you hollow.

She's not here. She's not anywhere. A digital ghost. And so she haunts.

The floor trembles beneath. Root-like veins gently spread toward the door. And once out there, they spread down the hall. Then down the steps, out the door to the building. And onto the street, toward the small downtown. Wood and carpet and concrete and blacktop, all shiveringly alive.

The wetness squishes in your ear and you follow the veins. Let 'em watch. Smashed beer bottles, mysterious stains on the cement, and discarded rotting food litter the street. The cacophony of smells and sensations isn't gone, just dimmed by her call.

On an empty street corner a few cops drive by, sirens blaring. Early for an emergency, or maybe late for one. Across the street, a park. Fairly empty, taking up a city block. Scattered park benches and some small grassy hills with a smattering of trees comprise the whole thing.

A couple early morning joggers and a few folks sleeping on the benches are all the life the park holds. But in the small cluster of woods you spot her.

Not scantily dressed, but in smart business wear. The kind that tries to suppress the passion, but can't quite conceal it. Or that's what you tell yourself at least. The blood swells. It now trickles from your ear. Her sound becomes crystal clear.

Heart palpitates like it's flip-flopping. Maybe

skips a beat every now and then from pounding too erratically, too powerfully. She doesn't notice you. But you want her to. But maybe you don't. Maybe it's better to know what she's doing. Or who she is. Or how she's even here.

This small city. Damn near the same block. *How*.

She spends a moment in the trees, the subtle glitch tracing after her movements. Mirroring them, but profane and unnatural. It's impossible to tell what she's doing. Suddenly she's off, walking quickly toward the other side of the park, her shadow too close and too far all at once. She's on the next block by the time you reach the edge of the trees. Hurried pace, but needing to keep some distance becomes the struggle.

Buildings grow more derelict as you get closer to the edge of the city. Not much life out here. Beyond is the oil-slick river surrounded by rows of dead and dying trees and piles of littered trash. Abandoned factories and crumbling warehouses. Remnants of a strong working class now diminished to little more than rust flakes and black & white photos that hang in the corner offices of the upper-middle class.

Bombed out, burned up; chewed and spat out. This is America.

Unsure if she's noticed you following or not, she gets lost in the cluster of industrial remnants. You hung back too much, let her get away. The fear sets in. So does the grief. Blood now flows from your ear for a moment before the cement ripples below and leads you closer, into one of the forsaken warehouses.

Dusty piles of rebar-penetrated cinder litter the vast roofless building. She disappears down a set of steps in the middle of the debris. Her shadow follows after, slightly delayed. Her movements strange and unnatural as she descends.

Glitchy and off. Worse and stranger than before.

As quietly as you can, you follow. Through the tattered warehouse and down the filthy steps. Her wetness echos in the darkness below. Moans raise the hairs on your neck.

The blood swells.

The blood also pours from your ear. Slick like oil

but quickly growing tacky like drying honey. Shirt soaked in thick red fluid and sweat. Ears full of wetness—both in sound and in blood.

Light on. A single room below the center of the massive building. Her room.

The bed she was on; same comforter, same antique brass frame headboard behind. Laptop sitting open. Hastily placed paintings. Lingerie and sex toys scattered around. A ravenous scent in the air.

Squishing and moaning, but the room is empty. A webcam sits on a desk near the edge of the bed. You go to look at the computer, for lack of knowing what else to do.

But the blood has been draining for so long. Lightheadedness damn near takes you to your knees. Head and eyes full of stars.

Reality rushes back and you're in your own room again. Nighttime. Laptop open and she's vibrating, skipping through space in that irreal way. Glitch but made flesh.

The blood pumps and swells. Ear still bleeding,

but it's of no consequence. She's here again. On screen it's a solo chat. No one else. No watchers, no annoying commenters. Just you and her.

Finally. You and her.

Part of you knows it makes no sense, but it also makes all the sense in the world. Everything you've ever wanted—wait, is this it? *Everything?* But the thoughts fade fast. She's on her knees, ass to the camera. Her neck strained so she can stare back at you—into you—at the same time. She's inviting you in. Open. Wet and warm and so comforting.

Yes. Everything you've ever wanted. *Everything.*

You sit down in front of her, blood swelling with a pressure previously unknown to your body. It fights against your veins and runs from your ear. Your face to the screen, up against her skin. But also actually up against her skin. It's bizarrely cold, but so warm and inviting. Watching yourself on the screen put your face in her ass. Also being the one on the screen—the one in the room—putting your face in her ass. The squishing sound permeating your every molecule.

The chill of her touch courses through your flesh and bones and muscle and blood. Sweet, hot blood. And it's swelling. So tight it might pop and leave you deflated on the ground of your filthy one room apartment, but also on the ground of her room. On the floor of the room on the screen.

And the way she moves, back and forth in an unknowable cadence. Mirroring her own movements. It makes no sense on the screen and it makes no sense in front of you in the room. But it worms through you, radiates out of you and you're doing it too. Both in your room and on the screen in front of you, as you watch yourself touch her. Splitting down the middle.

Fractured selves both existing in one feedback loop of boiling hot pleasure, chilling touch, and sensations so deeply embedded that they may never come out. It feels so fucking good. Like you could fuel the world with this energy if only it was catchable. Containable. Sensual and erotic, but beyond all that as well. Magnetic. Complete pole reversal. Negative to negative and positive to positive, but both repelling and attracting all at once. And the movement within that sticking close to you like a shroud.

Her moans move through your, shaking your core. Shattering a foundation deep within. You were right. There was a connection back there, on the screen before; now on the screen and in her room. Unspoken for fear of spoiling it. Unanswered for fear of ruining it.

But it's real. Her cold skin grinding against yours. The way you connect and disconnect and reconnect through so many channels like inputs and outputs. The floor below you ripples with pleasure waves in approximation with hers. You shift and lean into it, pushing further into her. Pressing against all her openness. Begging her to swallow you whole. To consume your very being so you can be united forever.

There is no resistance. She draws you in. Both the you in the flesh, pulled deeper and deeper into the cold crevasses of her body, and also the you in your apartment, pulled deeper into the screen; plastic cracking and adjusting, stretching to make room to fit all of you.

Both halves are pulled further in and down, below the known worlds. Somewhere deep inside. The places that feed us and teach us and give us gifts like fear and passion. Below the confines of knowledge and understanding. One half fleshy and cold. The other half plastic and hot. A tangle of slick wires. A plasma-coated chamber. Both breathe and pulse. Both hum and squish and moan. Both are salvation and comfort.

In both, we are home.

LEAD THE BLIND
JUSTIN LUTZ

You find the bar easily enough, a brick facade scratched with graffiti, a door covered in faded and peeling stickers, neon signs glowing behind the grated windows. Looking around, the street is empty, draped in an unnatural silence. Your hand hesitates on the handle, though only for a second, and you wrench the heavy door open and step inside. Cool and dark, cavelike, music crackling from hanging speakers, distorted guitars, muffled bass, the tinny snap of a snare drum.

You want to appear confident, like you know what you're doing, are in control of your life, so you walk quickly to a stool and prop your forearms on the bartop. Your foot beats a rhythm against the rung of the stool.

A surly bartender with tattoos half obscured by a ratty flannel shirt and facial hair that looks half intentional tosses a cardboard coaster like a frisbee. It settles in front of you and he gestures to you with his chin.

"Know what you're havin'?"

You know what you're supposed to order, know what you came here to do, but you stumble, eyes darting to the chalkboard behind the row of bottles, scan until you find something familiar, a bobbing buoy in this sea of uncertainty.

"Sure, how about the, uh, the Hunter Thompson?"

All the drinks in here are named after dead writers and dead directors, a chalkboard roster of debaucherous creatives.

The bartender narrows his eyes, shrugs like *whatever, fuck it*, and starts assembling the elements for your drink. A bloody mary, topped with a sausage; a cup of coffee, a sliced grapefruit. Based on some off the cuff remark, surely intended to shock and titillate, that the late writer made of his preferred breakfast. You're thankful this bar doesn't insist on the margaritas and cocaine.

"We sell most of these in the morning," the bartender says, skewering a sausage on a wooden stick and dunking it into the tomato juice. You look to the clock on the wall, suddenly embarrassed. He sets the drinks in front of you, starts halving the grapefruit.

"Oh, well," you say, stammering, knowing you've made the wrong choice, that this chance is blown, "I heard about it and wanted to try it."

"Uh huh," the bartender says, plunking the grapefruit down in front of you. "Enjoy your breakfast, Hunter." He shuffles down the bar to attend to someone else and you pick at the sausage sticking out of your drink, discouraged and alone.

The following day you find the same bar, open the same heavy door, sit down in front of the same grizzled bartender. He seems to have either slept in his clothes or never left, stands behind the bar as a slightly more rumpled version of the man you met yesterday.

"Are you here for your mid-afternoon grapefruit?"

He asks, tossing the coaster, something that must be his signature move.

"Ha," you laugh, "not today. Shot and a beer?"

He disappears and you curse yourself, know that you fucked it up again. What's so hard about the words, what's so hard about asking?

In here a shot and a beer is called a Charles Bukowski.

A glass clunks in front of you and the bartender cracks the beer open, grabs the whiskey bottle. "Hey, so actually," you start, and something holds you back yet again, something stills your tongue. He waits, bottle in hand, doesn't want to waste the shot while you waffle. You gesture to him that you still want the whiskey. He pours it and slides it across the bar, sets the sweating beer next to it.

Taking the shot, your throat burns and your palms sweat. You found this bar, dug it out after weeks of hearing about it, fiending for it, so why the streak of cowardice?

You push the shotglass back to him and he starts

to pour again and the liquor buoys your courage and before you know it the words are pouring from your mouth.

"Actually, hey, could I also get a Lucio Fulci?"

He locks eyes with you, the glass overflowing and leaking onto the bar. His eyes narrow and he stoppers the bottle, takes the shot himself. "You sure about that?"

You nod, sheepish, drain half your beer in one gulp.

The bartender sighs. "We blind-"

"-see things more clearly," you say, the line you read about, the response practiced in the mirror.

"Alright, man," the bartender says, pouring you each another shot. He nods to your beer. "You can bring that."

He looks around the barroom, confirms that the other patrons aren't looking up at the bar, and waves his fingers at you. You stand from your stool, grab your beer, your guts in turmoil with nerves and anxiety. Something guitar based pulses from the speakers, a riff that repeats and threatens to drive you mad. You've been preparing for this, but are you ready?

Heavy feet live at the end of your legs, you lift them each in turn and continue to the end of the bar. The bartender continues down a hallway toward the bathrooms and you follow, pause for him to unlock a third unmarked door. Behind it is another hallway, this one shorter, one door at its terminus.

"You're sure you did this on purpose, that this is what you want?" He asks. You nod and he sighs. "Alright, man."

He unlocks and opens the door and you both step into a dimly lit room. Closing the door behind you, the bartender clicks the wheel on a lamp and the room glows slightly brighter. The shade is translucent, basking the entire room in red. Sparsely populated, the main occupant of the space is a pedestal near the back wall, something covered with a crimson sheet. A laundry hamper sits pushed against the left wall and he gestures to it. "You can put your clothes in there."

"What?" you ask. This part of it you didn't know about, weren't expecting.

"Trust me," he says, "you're going to want to be

nude for this." He points across the room at a door you don't see until now. "When you're done, there's a shower in there."

He grips your shoulder, a weird and unexpected gesture, then leaves through the door you entered from.

For a moment you're not sure what to do so you stand alone, staring at the pedestal, completely frozen by fear, anxiety, and indecision. This is what you came here for, though, what you heard about and sought out, so you shirk your shirt, unbuckle your belt and slide off your pants. Naked, vulnerable, you stand in the red glow and feel shame like you've never experienced. No one knows you're here. You're not sure what the bartender will expect for the bill, but you have an idea, a figure whispered to you by strangers. Your skin breaks out in goose pimples, your dick sucks back into your body in retreat, not wanting to hang out for whatever this next part will be. It occurs to you that you shed your clothes so easily on the word of a bartender, that he could have cameras in this room and the staff could be laughing at you, gawking at you, hanging you out to dry in the back room of a dive bar.

You're here, you're committed, so you take a few steps forward and pull the sheet from the pedestal.

◉

It's Brian that first tells you about the bar, the back room. You've been looking for something new, something exciting, some weird ass new thing in this boring city you live and work in. Ennui has set in and it's crushing, grueling, untenable, so over drinks you ask Brian if maybe it's time to leave and he tells you about the unmarked door, the bar with no sign out front.

"I hear," he says, slamming the last half of his beer, "that's it's completely wild. Like nothing you've ever seen."

"You hear? You mean you haven't gone?"

"Well, no," he says, waving his glass at the bartender, signaling for another, stalling for time, "but I've seen it confirmed."

"Seen it confirmed? What's back there?" You ask.

Brian accepts his new beer with a nod, sips from the top, wipes foam from his upper lip. "Transcendence."

Under the sheet is a glass jar, almost a foot wide. Liquid fills it nearly to the top and swimming in the clear sea behind the glass are eyes; different colors and shapes, some with the optical nerve still trailing from the back of them like a tail. Most are white, some are bloodshot, crisscrossed with lightning veins and astigmatisms and cataracts. Next to the jar, a small knife, its handle black plastic and the blade dagger-like, threatening.

You're shaking, unsure you want to go through with this, but when you turn and try the knob on the door it's locked. You pound on the wall, shout until your voice goes hoarse, then stand there panting, sweating, naked, and look back to the jar.

Each of the eyes has a life of its own, swims back and forth in the liquid like a tadpole. Like sperm. Like something seeking to be born, clamoring for the way into this world.

Slowly, hands shaking, you take the top from

the jar and set it on the pedestal next to the knife. Your hand hovers above the surface of the liquid and the eyeballs congregate, fight for the surface like fish waiting to be fed. Remembering that you brought your beer in here, you pluck it from the floor next to the hamper and chug the rest of it, steel your nerve, wish you had more whiskey.

Without meaning to, you make eye contact with one of the floating orbs, the iris a faded green. Divorced from the heads they used to live in, the eyes don't blink, instead capturing you in an uncanny and disconcerting staring contest. Coming in here, you're not sure what you're supposed to do, weren't ever told what would happen when you order the Fulci, breach the back room, end up here. You figure the knife is clear enough, so again you go to the jar, stand with your naked torso and pelvis reflected in the glass. You think again of cameras, of being watched, how the eyes are a perfect weird symbol of the potential voyeurism.

With your hand over the jar, the eyes smash into one another near the surface, fight for your attention, and instead of actively choosing you look up to the ceiling and plunge your hand into the jar.

Inside, the liquid is warmer and more soothing than you expect. You don't look but can feel the eyes rubbing against the skin of your hand, can feel the optic nerves twist and snake around your fingers. You think of squeezing your hand shut, clenching each eye in turn so hard that the whites burst in your hand like a soft boiled egg, the warm goo inside each coating your fingers.

Instead you turn your hand and cradle your fingers, slowly pulling out of the jar and straining the liquid. When your hand breaks the surface and is in the open air again you look down and see that one eye has emerged victorious, the one with the faded green iris and long, searching optical nerve. It rolls in your palm, looking around the room and pulling itself across your fingers using the dangling tentacle.

Mesmerized, you stare at it for a long time, ask yourself impossible questions. Can it live in the air? Does it breathe water? Does it breathe? Why does it seem alive? None of these questions have answers, and no answer would be satisfying.

What's back there, you asked Brian.

Transcendence.

It's a minute, an hour, a day, no way to know, and you remember the knife. It feels natural in your hand when you pick it up, and somehow you know what to do, know what you're supposed to do, know what you need to do. Holding the knife by the black plastic handle, you bring it to your face, position it in the corner of your right eye socket.

Whiskey and beer roil in a storm in your belly, your testicles pull up tight against your pelvis. There's nothing natural about this and everything in your body is fighting you to take the knife away, don't harm us, don't do it don't do it don't-

Before you can talk yourself out of it you drive the point of the knife into the side of your eye socket. Instantaneous pain fills your head and face and blood drips down your cheek like a thick red tear. Falling to the ground, the knife still sticks out of your socket like a flagpole, like conquered ground. You close your hand around the eye from the jar, don't want to lose it, or worse: drop it and fall on it, squelching all the hidden wonder from it. You're not sure why but this eye is very important, this eye has chosen you, found you, sought you out, and you must protect it at all cost.

Lying on the ground, you raise a shaking hand to your face and touch the handle of the knife, sending a new wave of pain through your skull. You take a deep breath, count to three, and with the heel of your hand you push the knife sideways toward your nose and free the eye from your face. You howl in pain, clutch the socket and let the knife and liberated eye both fall to the concrete. On your knees, you keel over and vomit, the regurgitated booze mixing with the growing puddle of blood on the floor.

Unable to think straight, unsure what you're even doing, you pick up your eye, your dead eye, and stand, shaking and naked. You reach to the jar and drop it in, the bloody organ turning the liquid in the jar a pale pink, tendrils of blood wisping off of the desecrated eye like smoke. Unlike the others, your eye sinks to the bottom of the jar and rests there, a mutilated and cast off reject, an enemy.

In your left hand is still the eye you plucked from the jar, and without knowing why you raise your hand to your face and open your fingers. The questing optic nerve finds your bloody socket and penetrates it, worms around inside like inspecting a house before moving in. Using the tentacle the eye crawls into your face and secures itself there, your face symmetrical once again. Instantly a wave of nausea sweeps through you and you vomit again, slipping around in your own mess. Your equilibrium feels off and you try to stand, try to get control of yourself, and then you open the lids on your new eye and the room is gone.

You stand, if you're still standing, in murky gray, a sheet of fog that fills your vision and coats everything around you. Initially lost, you turn your head, looking for a landmark, wave your hands, then the fog begins to dissipate and something inside you lets you know that you're still in the room, you never left, this is just your new eye adjusting. You aren't sure how a disembodied eye could connect to your nervous system, but you decide that that's the least of your worries, might not be the weirdest thing you've experienced today.

Coming back to yourself, you raise your hands in front of your face, see they're coated in blood, remember the bartender's words: *you're going to want to be nude for this*. You look down at your naked body, the puddles of blood and vomit on the floor, look up to the pedestal with its ghoulish jar full of eyes, every one of them looking at you, all except the one you dropped in. Your freed eye rests on the bottom of the jar, a dead organ cloaked in swirling pink.

Something in the corner of your vision moves and you turn your head too fast, your newly oriented sight shaking and wobbling, causing nausea to rise in your belly.

When you're done, there's a shower in there.

You cross the room to the door and the eyes follow you, swim in the murky liquid to train on your naked body. For a moment you consider throwing the sheet back over the jar, concealing them, wonder if they'll sleep like a tropical bird, then twist the knob and all but fall into the bathroom. There's no toilet, no sink; the room is a tight square and every surface doubles as part of the shower stall. Eye level on the wall above the shower controls is a small mirror that you assume is for shaving. You bend to examine your new eye, pull at the skin of your cheek, roll the foreign organ around in your face.

Again there's something in the corner of your perception, some wraith that skirts your vision, and you spin in the small room, see nothing there, no one here with you. Your eyes end up back in the mirror and standing directly behind you is a man, about your height, disheveled and naked. In his face is a hole, a gaping black maw where one of his eyes used to be, and his remaining eye is glazed over but somehow still sears into you, stares with a focus you wouldn't think possible, and warm piss drips down your leg. Shaking, you turn again, ready to punch this stranger in the face, ready to tear and rip and grab and pull but there's nothing, no one.

You stand in a puddle of piss for a few moments, breathing heavily and scanning the room, then turn on the shower and step in.

When you step out into the room with the eyeball jar, there's an eyepatch among your clothes.

Leaving the back room, the front of the bar is empty, the stools tipped upside down on the bartop and the whole place reeking of bleach. You stumble out the front door and the world outside is dark, a deep dark transitioning to the hazy glow of dawn, and you wonder how long you were back there, how you could have possibly spent hours. Horns honk their defiance in the street, vents steam disappointment into the open air, the babble of human speech fights for the space in your ears.

You're wearing the eyepatch, and since putting it on haven't seen another wraith, no eyeless men lurking in the corners of your vision. You have to get home, need to sleep, need to wash the stench of the bar and the eyes and the blood and the ghosts from you despite your recent shower.

You expect everyone to notice you, to look askance at the hobbling man with the eyepatch, expect them to be able to somehow still see the blood you scrubbed from your skin, smell the piss you left behind in the bar. No one even looks up, so many eyes staring only at the ground, the street, the next step ahead of them.

Neon lights flash in your eyes, their tails swimming when you turn your head. Somehow, despite the hour, the streets are crowded, bodies bumping into your shoulders and your breath getting shallow and labored with the effort and the strain.

You have to get home.

Your depth perception is skewed, strange, and you lurch around the sidewalk like a drunk. You want to pull off the eyepatch, let the roaming organ behind the cotton shroud correct your vision and your gait, but you think of the wraith in the bathroom and leave it in place.

Almost home now, two more blocks, and someone bumps into you so violently that you fall to the ground, land on the rough sidewalk and scuff your palms.

"Hey, watch where you're going, buddy!"

You start to stand, start to yell, but already a fist is reaching out to catch you in the face, and the man's watchband snags the strap of your eyepatch and pulls it off of your head.

A grey mist fills the sides of your vision, but when you stand you feel instantly more sure, more correct, more stable.

We blind see more clearly.

You scan for your assailant, ready to fight back, punch him in the mouth, but if he's here he's just another face in a faceless crowd, a number among the rabble. Instead, the crowd ripples and you think you see something grey in the crowd, a pale figure in the throng, then people split and you see him, the man from the mirror, his empty socket leaking blood down his face and neck.

No one seems to notice him there, and for a moment you feel insane, out of your mind, but how is this figure any more unbelievable than a jar of eyes in the back of a dive bar?

The two of you stand and stare through the crowd, your good eyes locking and your new one honing in on his empty socket. You can sense something coming from him, a longing, a hunger pulsing off of him in waves. You're repulsed, angry, and in this moment you know that he's come for his eye.

"You can't fucking have it, it's mine!" You shout, and only one person looks up from their walking, everyone else shuffles by, your screams no more strange than any other day.

You can't stand this thing, this wraith, this ghost staring at you so you advance, push through the crowd and ignore grunts of disapproval. The wraith doesn't turn, doesn't run, doesn't move, stands staring with its one eye, waiting for you. At first you're not sure you're getting any closer and aren't sure what you'll do when you reach him, you just know that this is an imperative, you have to let him know that this eye is yours, yours, you fished it from the jar, you mutilated your own face, you own it now and you see through it and it's yours-

You reach the wraith and reach out to strike it, expect your hands to sink through his ashy, grey, translucent visage, but your hands hit something solid. You can't believe that you connect, that your hands meet flesh, so you shove as hard as you can and there's a thick and sickening sound like packing meat and the hiss of air brakes and screams from the sidewalk.

Startled, almost too stunned to move, you realize that the eyepatch is in your clenched fist, maybe never left you, so you stretch the band around your head and cover your new eye.

Looking into the street, you see a stopped city bus and in front of it is a woman, her body splayed at an impossible angle, blood leaking from her head and her purse exploded like a pinata, personal effects surrounding her in grisly tableau.

All around you you hear speculation, the attention of the city finally grabbed by something so over the top and awful that it has no choice but to take notice.

"I think someone pushed her."

"Did you see who it was?"

"She was jaywalking."

"That driver is fucked."

No one is looking at you, all eyes fixated on the blood in the street, so you slip back into the crowd and take the last two blocks home at the most inconspicuous pace you can manage, your heart hammering in your chest.

Third time at the bar, third time through the door, third time seeing the scruffy bartender in the flannel shirt. This time he nods at you, doesn't crack a joke, doesn't offer a drink recommendation, just tosses coasters to you and Brian and stands with his fists on the bartop.

"Okay, so how do I do this?" Brian asks.

"Dude." I shake my head, order a beer and a shot, and the bartender floats off to fetch it. "You can't act like that, it's not a joke."

"Well it sure seems like it's not that serious, and you won't tell me what fucking happened to your eye, so maybe I want to see for myself," he says.

You went to Brian after the bar, the bus, the woman in the street, but you tell him none of it except that you found it, it worked, but you don't have any more answers. He insists on coming with you to the bar, finding it for himself.

Returning, the bartender slides you your shot, cracks the beer with a flat bottle opener, then turns to Brian.

"I'll have a Fulci," Brian says, eyes gleaming, face split in a grin.

"You got it," the bartender says, and turns to the row of bottles, pulls down a gin.

Brian turns to you and winks, nearly slobbering. The bartender pours some things into a glass, fills it with ice, stirs with a metal bar spoon. When he sets the drink in front of Brian you don't know what to say, what to do, so you look on with your good eye, expression deadpan.

"What the hell is this?" Brian picks up the drink, sips it, makes a face.

The bartender shrugs. "It's basically a negroni, I

just-"

"No," Brian interrupts, "I mean what the hell *is* this, I thought that was the secret word, the code or secret handshake or whatever the fuck."

Narrowing his eyes, the bartender pours you another shot, never looking away from Brian. "Respectfully, man, I don't have a clue what you're talking about."

Brian's eyes dance between you and the bartender. "You guys are fucking assholes, fuck both of you." He picks up the drink, drains it in one long pull. He points a sweaty finger at you, eyes wild. "You're fucking paying for that." He shakes his head, stands, makes a show of pushing the stool in. "Keep your secret club or whatever, you two can get fucked."

Brian storms out, the heavy door settling into the jamb with a heavy *wum*p, sealing you in with the bartender, the two of you alone for a third time.

"Why didn't it work for him?"

Looking up, the bartender pours himself a shot, clinks it into yours, drains it. He shrugs. "I can tell when someone is pure of intention, when they really mean it. Plus," another shot, "it changes depending on what you're looking for. That wasn't his drink."

You sit in silence, whiskey burning the back of your throat. You stare with your good eye into the mouth of your beer can, want to climb into the aluminum void, curl up at the bottom, drown.

"I want to take it back," you say.

"No refunds."

"I didn't pay anything," you say, bringing the beer to your lips. "I want this thing gone, and I want mine back." You pull the patch from your eye, glare at him with both your good one and your glazed grey one, slip it back in place before the wraith can appear in the corner of your vision.

"Fuck, man, keep that thing under wraps in here, please," he says. You see sweat break out on his forehead, watch his eyes dart around in their sockets. When the patch is securely in place he pours each of you another shot. "You want a grapefruit?"

You know he's joking, trying to make light of the

situation, but you're fed up, can't stand it. All night you toss and turn, dreaming of wraiths and dead women in the street, screaming strangers, dirty men with filthy fingernails trying to scoop out your eye.

"I want to go back there again. I'll have a Fulci."

"I'm telling you man, that's not how it-"

Before he finishes his sentence you're off the stool, around the bar, opening the door to the hallway. His cries follow you but you don't stop, don't turn, keep on the familiar path toward the room with the eyes. If you find the jar you can find your eye, fish it back out, replace it, make everything go back to normal. You don't want answers, don't want to see anything in the periphery of your vision, don't want specters haunting your days.

Bursting through the door you see there's no pedestal, no hamper, no jars, no eyes. You rush into the shower room, find it empty.

"What the fuck, where are they?" You scream, reentering the barroom. Behind the bar, the scruffy bartender shrugs again, starts to say something, but you cut him off. "I want my eye back, I want to fix it, reverse it, whatever."

"Man, I'm telling you, that's not how any of this works."

"Then tell me, how the fuck does this work?"

Before he can answer your faculties leave you and you pounce, knock him to the floor and straddle his torso, hold his arms to the ground. He struggles underneath your weight but you hold him down, your fury outweighing him. Your right arm paws around behind the bar, looks for something, anything, comes up with a corkscrew.

The bartender screams and you tear free your eyepatch, beckon the wraith, invite him in for this, want him to see it. Entering at the corner of your vision, he floats into the room, settles in front of you, good eye fixed on the writhing bartender, open socket weeping.

"We blind," you say.

"See more clearly," the wraith responds.

With the specter watching, you plunge the corkscrew into the meat of the bartender's eye and begin to twist.

MISBEGOTTEN
BRENDAN VIDITO

Hours—uncounted, unnoticed—had passed since Noah woke in the empty room, his throat and sinuses thick with the taste of blood and gunpowder. Cross-legged on the concrete floor, he kneaded his cheeks and forehead with uncertain fingers. The flesh was unreal, incongruent with his memory of how the shell had burst his head apart in a hail of bone and shredded meat. He traced a line down the middle of his brow, along one side of his nose, and under the curve of both cheekbones, where he remembered—or thought he remembered—the skin splitting and blooming outward like some grotesque flower opening its petals.

Since waking, the same thoughts circled through

his mind. Had he taken his own life? Or was this room and the memory of his suicide nothing but an elaborate delusion? If not, then what was this place and how had he come to be here? No matter how often he turned these questions over, or how much he obsessed over every facet and detail, no answers were forthcoming. Every attempt at rationalization was stifled by a voice in the margins of his awareness. A voice that repeated four words he could not ignore: *You should be dead. You should be dead...*

The caged bulb on the ceiling stuttered and buzzed. Noah looked up, starved for stimulation. Pale blue light flickered across the walls and steel door, which loomed—dented and scratched as though by fist and fingernail—a few paces in front of him. A beat. And the bulb resumed its steady, silent radiance. Once again, the only sounds became the too-loud drum of his heartbeat and the steady rhythm of his breathing.

Noah sighed. For too long, he had waited for something, anything, to break the tedium of his confinement. But the room had remained infuriatingly static. Even pounding against the door and shouting for help had produced no results. The place, he had come to understand, was a prison.

He bowed his head and sank back into his memories. The only place he could escape to, albeit temporarily. His recollection turned, for the umpteenth time, to that morning several weeks ago when he had decided to pursue death in earnest.

It was the middle of winter. At a shabby hotel in a forgotten corner of the city. He waited alone in the hallway outside the conference room—some twenty minutes early—staring at the paper sign taped to the door. In bold type, it read: FIREARMS SAFETY COURSE.

Earlier that week, Noah had decided to end his life. Though the notion had percolated in his mind for almost a decade, it was the combined news of an impending layoff and the re-emergence of his illness from a period of remission that prompted him to bring his courtship with death to a decisive conclusion. Research and deliberation led him to believe that placing a shotgun in his mouth would be the most effective and painless method to achieve his goal. But first, he needed a weapon. And to make such a purchase—legally at least—he had to obtain a firearms license. No one—friends nor family—knew he was there. It was his own guarded secret.

The hotel was a grim portal into the final chapter of his existence. Wallpaper covered the walls—jaundiced yellow gridded with vague geometric patterns. It peeled in places. Long, curled tongues lapped the mould spores fouling the air. A cold wind whispered down the halls. The place felt alive but weary—a great beast in the twilight of its decline.

Noah found himself seated on a plastic chair in the conference room, anonymous among a crowd of twenty or so other participants. They represented all ages and backgrounds, each keeping to themselves and showing signs of fatigue from the early hour. The instructor was a middle-aged man with a goatee and bifocals that distorted his eyes as he scanned those in attendance.

His nose and ears were crimson from the cold.

Over the next several hours, his voice droned from the front of the room. To Noah, the words abstracted into a mindless wash of sound. His attention was elsewhere, suspended in a grey area between awareness and an empty daydream. He proceeded through the examination in an automatic stupor, his pen scratching answers he somehow internalized throughout his mental absence. And before he could notice the passage of time, he was outside again, the wind clawing at his face and hands. Everything, numb. The first part of his plan complete.

◆

A metallic clang fractured the silence. Noah started, jarred from his memories. The steel door was opening, swinging slow and heavy, toward him. A woman—short and wide-shouldered— stepped into the room. She wore loose maroon slacks and a beige vest open over a white button-down shirt. Her hair, more slate than black, was cut short, with a cleft in the middle of her brow that exposed the deep lines on her forehead. She stood motionless, watching him.

"Good morning, Noah. How are you feeling?"

Noah opened his mouth and closed it again. He had become estranged from speech. It was only after his second attempt that he managed to produce words. "Morning." It was intended as a question but emerged devoid of inflection.

"Bright and early," the woman said. The words sounded absurd and mocking in the windowless confines of that concrete chamber.

"Where am I?" Noah started to get up but stalled when he realized his legs were asleep.

"One thing at a time, Noah. I understand you must be confused. I will attempt, in short order, to bring as much clarity to your situation as I can."

She approached, held out her hand, and helped him to his feet. The gesture turned into a handshake. She introduced herself with a name that sounded like Naught or Knot. Noah was too overwhelmed to ask for clarification and simply shook her hand. "Would you care to follow me to my office?" she said. "It is more comfortable than this waiting space."

He nodded and limped toward the door.

Beyond the drab eternity of his prison, a hallway receded to darkness in both directions. The walls were panelled with rich, dark oak. Cube-shaped lights that shed an autumnal glow were embedded in the ceiling at regular intervals. The opposite side of the steel door, Noah could now see, was designed to match the panelled walls. When Naught pulled it closed behind them, it blended flawlessly with the hallway. The only sign that a door existed was a discrete black handle that could only be perceived when the light struck it from a certain angle.

Noah followed Naught down the hallway. How many other doors and concrete chambers did the walls conceal? Were others like him waiting inside? He thought he spotted a few other handles along the way but couldn't be sure. They were moving too briskly, and the lighting was unreliable. Once he thought he heard what sounded like an open palm weakly pounding the opposite side of the wall, but again, he couldn't be sure.

He doubted the evidence of his senses. Every breath in this place seemed tainted by a mild psychoactive agent, sowing seeds of paranoid doubt in the folds of his mind.

Naught veered to the right. And they were inside her office. A wide, rectangular room, the length of which was dominated by a panoramic window. The glass produced no reflection. Beyond, Noah perceived nothing but a flat, disorienting darkness. Various potted plants—their plastic sheen betraying their artificiality—lined the floor under the window. To the left of the room stood a water fountain. An umbrella of clear, prismatic water plumed and rained down into a square basin tiled in various shades of blue and pink. On the opposite side of the room, two plush leather armchairs faced one another, the space between them occupied by a glass table. Upon it steamed a pot of tea and two empty cups.

Naught gestured for Noah to take a seat. The leather was cool under his bare arms, the seat a reprieve after spending so much time on a concrete floor. Naught poured them each a cup of tea and handed the small, clay vessel to Noah, who placed it under his nose.

"It's chamomile. For the nerves."

Noah sipped. The warmth was soothing.

Naught lowered herself into the chair opposite his own, and said, "I suspect you understand, on an intuitive level at least, why you are here."

Noah cradled his tea, hesitant to voice the uncertain truth simmering in his mind. Here was his chance to lay his doubts to rest. "I—" he faltered. "I killed myself."

"Last night in your apartment. With a shotgun you purchased from the department store."

He swallowed. He had pulled the trigger while seated in the corner of the living room between the window and his writing desk. The place he had chosen long before as the scene of his demise. For months before that moment, when the sun drew low, he had taken a seat there and acquainted his body with the space. Closing his eyes, he focused on the cool caress of the walls, the warm, dry breeze from the baseboard heater. Over time the corner had become a surrogate womb, a place of comfort and security. A womb now washed with his blood.

He saw it now in his mind. A vast red supernova. Dense near the point of origin and expanding—halfway up the ceiling—in a violent, irregular cone. His body slumped and headless except for half the jawbone, which hung upon his chest by a strip of flesh and muscle. A gentle rain fell. Red dappled the floor around his legs. The papers scattered around his desk. Hissing as it struck the heater. Brain matter, slick and grey, clung to the nearby curtains. One of his teeth, broken above the root, rested on the windowsill.

Noah brought two fingers to his brow. "I remember my head coming apart."

"We have many aspects, Noah. You destroyed only one of them."

He set down his teacup. "Where am I?"

"In a space between."

"An afterlife."

She shook her head. "There is no such thing."

"Then what is this place?"

"You are inside my office. And my office is situated within a larger facility." Her voice was calm, unwavering. "We intercepted you after you had taken your own life."

"What does that mean?" Noah said. "And who is we?"

"We as in myself and my colleagues." She tilted her head as though to gesture to these unseen associates. "Think of us as benign interventionists. As for what our interception implies, I can only repeat what I have already told you. There are things—the nuisances and intricacies of reality, both perceptible and otherwise—that would be impossible to explain to you in the little time we have together."

"Please try."

"Noah, you are not built to understand," Naught said. "Let us focus instead on the tangibles. We are sitting together. Inside my office. You were brought here because I want to help you."

Noah slumped, head in his hands. "None of this makes any sense."

He was tired. So. Fucking. Tired. But how could that be? He was supposed to be dead. The discomfort, the anxiety, the negative emotions. Everything he was trying to escape coursed through him with renewed fervour. And all he wanted from the beginning was—

"Nothing," Naught said. "The darkness on the other side of the door."

Noah straightened, tear trails glistening on his cheeks. He found nothing strange about Naught's ability to peer inside his mind. Not after everything he had already experienced.

"That is what you wanted." Naught interlaced her fingers in her lap.

"Is there another reason to choose death?"

"Every suicide is an attempt at retroactive erasure," Naught said. She leaned in and placed a hand on his knee. "And that is precisely why you are here. I can offer you this erasure. You might believe your death will come as a relief to your loved ones, but that is rarely ever the case. I can spare you the pain of existing, and your loved ones the pain of your loss."

"I don't understand."

"I'm offering you the chance of never being born."

The answer struck him like a blow. He leaned back in his chair and let his gaze wander around the room. He settled on the darkness beyond the panoramic window. As he stared, a throbbing started behind his eyes and a headache took root in his skull, its pain concentrated along the spectral fault line trenched by the shotgun blast. He was numb, beyond confusion. His reason silent. Its throat slit by the unreality of his surroundings, by the stubborn persistence of his being.

"My family," he said. "When will they find me?"

"In three days," Naught said. "Your mother will begin to worry when you fail to answer her calls and text messages. They will reach out to your landlord and have him open the door. The smell will hit them first. Your mother will recognize the odour immediately because of her medical background, but her mind will put up a barrier, shielding her psyche from the trauma that awaits her. They climb the stairs. Your father sees the blood first. He stops, frozen. Your mother pushes against his back, chiding him for stopping, the anesthesia of shock beginning its work. Your father utters a single word. *No.* The landlord lets out a strangled gasp. Your mother rushes to your side, a high keening in her throat. She takes your hands, pulls your limp, nearly decapitated body away from the wall. In a fit of madness, she scoops handfuls of brain matter from the floor and places it on the ruin of your neck, trying to piece you back together—"

"Please stop."

Naught fell silent.

"Will they be all right?" His voice and hands shaking.

"Your mother will regress into infantilism, utterly broken. A combination of neglect and poor health will lead to her death five years from now. Your father will persist for several years more, alone, his mind gnawed by the early onset of hereditary dementia. During his brief periods of lucidity, he will wonder—until the day he passes—where he went wrong as a parent."

Noah sobbed. His throat tight and raw. His eyes

burning.

His mind flashed on a memory from his childhood. A morbid prank he had played on his mother. He had lain on the floor near the entrance, covered in theatre blood, the handle of a rubber knife taped to his chest. His mother screamed and cried when she arrived home from a trip to the grocery store. It was the only time she had ever laid a hand on him in anger. A quick, sharp slap across the face. *That's not funny, Noah*, she wailed. *Don't you ever do that again.*

The guilt he had experienced that afternoon was foundational. He would never forget what he had done, nor would he be able to erase his mother's screams from his memory. The slap had burned his cheek long after the blow was struck. And now, knowing how she would react to his suicide, that guilt surfaced anew, knife-edged and incandescent.

Noah reached out with languid, trembling hands, and Naught clasped them in her own. He squeezed them as sobs continued to rack his body. "Please. I want this to stop. I don't want to be here anymore. I'll do anything."

"I am here to help." Her voice was like water lapping his turbulent shores. "Your parents will never have to feel that pain. And you will not have to suffer in a body besieged by illness."

"What is it like? Never being born."

She smiled. "It is the nothing you seek. The darkness on the other side of the door."

His body relaxed. He released her hands and leaned back in his chair. He sniffed.

"Will it hurt?"

"No, Noah. Your pain is at an end."

Finally, the words he needed to hear.

"Okay." He nodded several times. "Okay, let's open that door together."

The office vanished with the abruptness of a dream. And Noah now found himself suspended in a void, like what lurked behind the panoramic window. He was naked and could only roll his eyes in their sockets. Beneath him, a bed or gurney, unseen, but felt—plush and soft—against his exposed skin. His ears were ringing, but otherwise, all was silence. He wasn't cold, and he wasn't afraid. A narcotic calm suffused and swaddled his mind and body.

Four figures stepped into his orbit of vision, two on each side. Clad in white, hooded robes, and featureless cloth masks that concealed their faces, they drew close, scalpels in hand. Without speaking, they began their work. One of them made an incision down Noah's chest, from sternum to groin. He registered no pain, nor did he sense any blood trickling across his skin. A second figure produced a gleaming retractor instrument and installed it near his midsection. A third figure stepped up behind the first and reached inside him, their shoulders working as they searched for some hidden prize within. After a moment, they took a step back, bringing with them an object, glimpsed on the fringes of Noah's vision. It was reddish brown, blurry, dripping, distorted by eyestrain, but even so he could tell for certain it was no organ he recognized.

With a wet peeling sound, two figures unravelled

the object like a scroll made of living flesh. Every action induced a pulling, jerking sensation deep in Noah's body. It wasn't painful, or uncomfortable, but he had the impression these figures were handling a part of him that could not be accessed while he was alive—an occultic mechanism forged of both flesh and spirit. They laid it out—a considerable length of it judging by how long it took to unfurl—across a platform outside Noah's line of sight.

The rest of the procedure transpired outside his purview. Sometimes, he heard a hissing sound, followed by the stench of something burning. Other times, a vibratory hum filled the air in anticipation of the red flash that would follow. These flashes occurred in an almost rhythmic fashion, and each time, a memory—long archived and rarely visited—streaked across his mind's eye. A random day in the backyard during his childhood. A quiet moment with an ex-girlfriend after waking up together in the morning. The sun casting long shadows during an evening stroll. These visitations were short-lived—no more than a frame in a flip book—before they retreated into the tunnels of his memory. Some of these flashes, however, upon fading, left him with a tremor of unease, a feeling of having forgotten something important. But the sensation was short-lived, superseded by the gentle delirium induced by the strangeness of his surroundings.

After a time, the procedure was complete. The figures had reinserted the scroll into his body. Mended his sundered flesh with a tool that resembled a shaft of quartz. And retreated into the void beyond the scope of his vision. Noah closed his eyes and waited for oblivion. He thought of his parents finding his body. Of the corner where he had taken his life. The fading hotel where ideation transgressed into action. All these memories would soon become fiction. Passages in a story forgotten to the grinding passage of time. *I'm so sorry*, he thought, addressing no one and everyone. *I'm sorry for all the pain I caused.* He opened his mouth and uttered one final goodbye—two notes cast like bottled messages into the darkness. Noah breathed the last air he would ever breathe and waited for oblivion…

❖

Hours—uncounted, unnoticed—had passed since Noah woke in the empty room, his throat and sinuses thick with the taste of blood and gunpowder. Cross-legged on the concrete floor, he kneaded his chest and stomach with uncertain fingers. The flesh was unreal, incongruent with his memory of how the robed figures had opened his body to work on some unknowable organ. He traced a line between his breasts, around his navel, and down to where his pubic hair began, where he remembered—or thought he remembered—the skin parting like a door into his spiritual viscera.

Since waking, the same thoughts circled through his mind. Why had he returned to this room? What happened to never being born? Had Naught deceived him, or was there a part of this process he did not understand? No matter how often he turned these questions over, or how much he obsessed over every facet and detail, no answers were forthcoming. Every attempt at rationalization was stifled by a voice in the margins of his awareness. A voice that repeated five words he could not ignore: *Why are you still here? Why are you still here?*

He stood and walked to the door, slamming his fist against the metal surface.

"I need to speak to Naught. Please. Something is wrong."

His cry echoed throughout the oubliette and assaulted his eardrums. He pounded the door again, renewing his assault until he couldn't hold his arm up anymore. Whimpering, he turned and paced the room, hoping one of his circuits would reveal the door opening. The bulb on the ceiling flickered and buzzed and he screamed at it, incoherent and hysterical, spittle flying from his lips. Finally, his exertions had taken their toll and he collapsed, crawling on the floor until even that became too much, and he flattened himself on his stomach, cheek against the cold concrete, weeping in exhausted bursts. Sleep came, eventually— an assassin stalking up behind to open his throat. His awareness irised into nothingness, and he escaped one prison only to enter another.

◆

The room was familiar. Small but comfortable, a swaddle of walls and candy-coloured furniture. The curtains—patterned with cartoon dinosaurs—were pulled over the window, and under it, a single bed, dressed in more prehistoric caricatures, held a boy of six or seven, his mouth hung open in sleep. A star projector on the bedside table cast a multicolour nebula across the ceiling.

Noah stood in the far corner, near the closet door, coming to the slow realization that he was inside his childhood bedroom. And the boy in the bed was a younger version of himself. Was this a dream? A memory? He looked down at his hands; he was able to move them. He examined the palms and veins threaded across the dorsal side. The air in the room was also dense with his juvenile presence, a sweaty, earthy odour blended with the lemon scent of his mother's cleaning products. The smell struck him with a nostalgic blow. The scene was all too real.

He approached his dresser and examined the framed photograph on it. In it, a pale, sickly Noah of a year or so prior. He lay on the family couch, covered to the waist in a blanket. His cat, Lucas—now long deceased—slumbered in his lap, ever the caring presence. The animal had always sensed when he wasn't feeling well and had remained by his side for over a decade—his proximity a balm whenever the burden of Noah's illness became too much for him to carry. He smiled at the photo now and mouthed his thanks to the animal.

A sound pulled his attention away from the photograph. A sharp intake of breath from somewhere behind him. He turned, still holding the frame. His younger self was sitting upright in bed, staring not at him, but the open door to the bedroom. The star projector, programmed to cycle through various colour combinations, had stalled on a deep crimson—not unlike the red flashes Noah had seen during the surgical procedure in the void. The hue bathed the walls and ceiling and sharpened the shadows on young Noah's horrified expression. What was he looking at? Noah couldn't see from this angle, but he assumed, whatever it was, stood framed in the doorway. He stepped closer to the bed, adjusting his vantage point, and froze—his veins filling with panic and dread—when the thing came into view. The photograph slipped from his hand.

A pale shape—tall and wide enough to fill the doorframe—stood immobile, gazing down at the young Noah with empty, shadowed sockets. It was humanoid, but in a fashion that was derisive—a parody of form and semblance. Lumpen, white flesh. The impression of a gaping mouth, though it was impossible to discern its features with any certainty. The thing was wreathed in a distorting haze, as though caught between the corporeal and ethereal.

The young Noah opened his mouth and attempted to cry out, though no sound emerged. And watching his lips, his older counterpart read the word: *mom, mom, mom*. A refrain echoed like a record skip as the boy sat there, frozen and terrified. The older Noah tried to move, to intervene, but he too was frozen. His body leaden and inoperable. As though his abilities ceased to function in the presence of this abnormality, this wrongness made flesh.

Had this encounter occurred at some point in his history? He cast his mind back, trying to recall the sighting of such a creature. Did it occur in a nightmare or illness-induced delusion? There was a seed of recollection, buried deep in the folds of his mind, an impression of fear, but he couldn't tell for certain. The present moment could also be colouring his past, and this encounter was not a dream or memory, but something else. Something far worse than any nightmare.

Noah—both the young and old—watched, helpless, as the entity emerged from the doorway and approached the bed. Its movements—like the rest of it—were unnatural: a stop-motion stutter as though it existed in a series of disjointed frames. In a matter of seconds, it loomed over the mattress, its shadow falling over the young Noah, chasing the red light from his features. The older Noah somehow knew that his younger self had released the contents of his bladder. He remembered, or intuited, the warmth as it washed between his legs and soaked into the sheets. The entity reached out with one gnarled hand—like a lump of clay appended with three misshapen digits—and made a grab for the boy. At the last second, volition returned to his body, and he dove toward the floor. But the hand locked around his ankle and dragged him back and up so that he hung upside down inches away from the thing's face.

The entity lowered its head and the boy's arm disappeared into its mouth. Muscles worked. The snapping of bone broke the silence. And a scream wrested, at last, from the victim's throat. It was high and genderless, an animalistic wail heard only upon the precipice of death. The older Noah screamed too, though only in his mind. There were no words to describe the unnatural horror of watching one's younger self in a state of extremis. It sickened every cell in the body. Shattered every preconception of right or wrong, real and unreal. Tears sprung to his eyes, and he couldn't avert his gaze, no matter how hard he willed himself to turn away.

The entity chewed the boy's arm off at the shoulder. Dark, arterial blood poured from the wound. A deathly pallor suffused his skin. His eyes glazed over, and his mouth hung open in a look of idiotic dismay. He had stopped screaming and instead resumed mouthing a silent appeal for their mother. The next mouthful claimed one shoulder and half his torso. His organs, now liberated from their chassis, unravelled and slopped to the floor, filling the room with the stench of blood and shit. The entity chewed. Flesh squelched. Bones cracked. And cartilage popped. In little time, the boy had been utterly consumed.

Noah stared and stared and stared. Eyes wide. Mouth open. Every part of him sick and numb and shattered with horror. The entity stood before him, sated, baptized in blood, its jaw still working in lazy circles. As Noah continued to watch, it twitched, convulsed, and finally turned to look at him. Its shadowed, eyeless sockets bore through skin and muscle and bone. To the very core of his being, tasting the saccharine terror that festered there. In an instant, the leaden weight fell from his body, and Noah could think of nothing else but to open his mouth and—

He woke screaming and thrashing on the concrete floor. His clothes were heavy with cold sweat and his jaw ached from clenching his teeth. His unconscious spasms had scraped the skin from his elbows and blood smeared the concrete in frenetic half-circles. After a time, his screams diminished to a hoarse whimper and he lay completely still, staring at the ceiling.

What had he been dreaming about? What could have possibly instilled so much fear in him? He searched his memory, but the threads of the nightmare were evaporating like sun-warmed mist. A faded image of his childhood bedroom. Red light. And nothing more.

He tried to remember his past as a boy of six

or seven—when his bedroom had aligned with the impression from his nightmare—but came up empty. There was a gap in his personal history, a chasm where his early years should have been. How could he have forgotten so much? Was it this place? Was it eroding his memories? What did he look like at that age? What were his interests? What formative experiences had he accrued? The longer he puzzled about these absences, the more frustrated he became until—furious and confused—he climbed to his feet and paced the room. Circuit after circuit he marched, pounding on the door every time he passed.

He thought about how he wasn't hungry or thirsty. He thought about the other doors he had glimpsed in the hallway outside, and how he was likely not the only prisoner here. He thought about Naught and her lies, the failed promise of un-birth. He circled. And circled. And circled. Until he collapsed near the door, his head roaring with unanswered questions. Sleep found him again—a sinkhole opening in his skull—and he retreated grudgingly into its depths.

☩

His ex-girlfriend, Jordan, beckoned him down a forested path at dusk. Disoriented, he frowned in her direction, wondering where he was, when he was. Before he could say anything, though, a second Noah came up behind and jogged toward Jordan. She crossed her arms over her chest and laughed her musical laugh. This second Noah was in his early twenties, still in college, and the healthiest he had ever been in his life. At that time, the disease had slunk away into remission, and he had enjoyed the uninhibited freedom of young adulthood. Three months later, though, Jordan would leave him, and the disease would return. And along with it, the nagging ideation of suicide—a spectre that hung at intervals over his existence.

"You're fucking hammered," Jordan said, slapping Noah on the shoulder.

"Hammered and horny," he slurred. "Want to fool around when we get back to the trailer?"

"If you don't have whiskey dick, then, yeah, sure."

He blew a raspberry. "Dude, I'm ready to go."

"Let's focus on getting to the trailer first," Jordan said, threading her arm through his.

The older Noah—only four years the other's senior—followed close behind. He hadn't thought of Jordan in a while and realized—with a pang—that he missed her. She had always been kind and funny. Even when they were having problems. Not long after this summer retreat, a prestigious university would offer her a scholarship abroad, and she would accept. Noah had been concerned about his health overseas, the lack of free health care, and agreed—after a string of sleepless nights—that their parting was the right decision. He remembered holding her while they were parked outside his apartment. The radio was silent, and they listened to one another breathing. When he finally pulled away, he kissed her, quick and hard, and exited the vehicle.

He never saw her again. Until now.

The trailer came into view. A rusted, hulking thing owned by Jordan's eccentric uncle. As they approached the door, Noah disengaged from Jordan's arm and stumbled toward the bushes.

"What are you doing?" Jordan said.

"I have to take a leak. I'll meet you inside."

"All right. Try not to piss on yourself."

He saluted her and unbuckled his belt. She laughed, opened the trailer door with a screech of rusted hinges, and stepped inside. Rancid yellow light poured onto the grass, lighting the forest dark, before the door clapped shut behind her.

Noah watched from several paces away. His younger self aimed his stream at a patch of nettles and sighed as steam rose into the cool night air. He whistled a tune in a broken key, interspersing the notes with the occasional burp. Noah, the observer, shook his head, his laughter mingling joy and sorrow as he mourned the optimism he once possessed. If only things had been different, he thought. If only he could have found happiness.

A branch snapped in among the bushes. Both Noah and his younger twin looked up. A paleness delineated itself against the sprawl of stars, towering eight feet or more. It was human-like, but bulbous and distorted beyond any true likeness. It shambled forward, the leaves wilting on their branches as it passed. Before the younger Noah could react, it crushed his head between its clay-like hands. Bone, blood, and grey matter shot out into the grass. The other Noah gasped, stepped back, lost his footing and sprawled, twisting his ankle.

The entity raised the flattened head, and its dangling body—still jetting a stream of urine—toward its mouth and began to feast. The crickets and the birds fell silent, and the only sounds became the crunch and spurt of macerated flesh.

Noah crawled backwards through the grass, heart hammering, nausea pushing acid into his throat. His ankle howled. But terror had rendered his voice silent. He wanted to cry out, to warn Jordan, but all he could do was crawl.

Blood-stained hiking boots were last to disappear down the thing's throat. Its neck bulged, muscles working to pull the corpse into its stomach. All Noah could think about was a snake swallowing its prey by inches. When it was finished, it began walking toward him, heavy with sustenance, yellowing the grass in its wake. Overhead, a celestial body glowed a dark crimson—familiar, ominous, and incongruous to this sky, or any on this earth.

Noah held out his hands in a warding gesture. Somewhere, in the night, a scream rang out. High pitched and wavering. He realized, as the entity came upon him, that the scream was his own.

The room again. Pacing along its concrete walls. His ankle was swollen, though he could not remember how he had sustained the injury. And that wasn't the only hole in his memory. His skull was riddled with them. Unwilling trepanations were performed whenever he faded from consciousness. His memory, the only place he could escape to, albeit temporarily, was becoming an unreliable crutch. His only dependable reality now was the four walls that contained him. Six steps on one side. Eight on the other. Bang on the door. Scream. Curse. Weep. Watch the light flicker. Six steps again. Then eight. And start again. And again. And again.

How many days, weeks, or months had passed? How many times had he resigned himself to exhaustion? Crawled across the grey sands of Lethe's banks. Remember something. Anything. His parents. He must have parents. Why couldn't he see them in his mind's eye? Friends. Family. His home. The world outside this prison. Why couldn't he fucking remember anything?

He stopped pacing and faced the wall.

"Remember," he said and pushed his forehead against the rough concrete.

He applied pressure until it hurt and pulled away.

"Remember." He knocked his head against the wall, not too hard, but hard enough to send a shock through his skull.

"Remember." He slammed his head this time and saw stars.

"Remember." Harder. Hard enough to make him dizzy.

"Remember." The skin on his forehead split and blood coursed into his eyes.

"Remember." He almost blacked out from the force of the bludgeoning.

"Remember." He was bracing his hands against the wall now.

"Remember." His face ran hot with blood.

"Remember." He screamed and felt the front of his skull cave in.

Everything went black.

Hours—uncounted, unnoticed—had passed since Noah woke in the empty room, his throat and sinuses thick with the taste of blood and gunpowder. Cross-legged on the concrete floor, he kneaded his forehead with uncertain fingers. The flesh was unreal, incongruent with his memory of how the front of his skull had collapsed against the cold concrete. He traced a line from his hairline to the middle of his brow, where he remembered—or thought he remembered—the skin collapsing as the bone beneath pushed into his brain.

The caged bulb on the ceiling stuttered and buzzed. And a sound he didn't recognize echoed across the walls of his prison. A high metallic whine. Mind empty of all thought, Noah looked up, mouth agape, and saw the door was now open. Framed in the doorway stood a pale, lumpen form. A thin dribble of saliva ran from its misshapen mouth. As Noah stared, a single word forced its way into the vacuum of his mind, a name he heard in a dream, or another life: Naught.

Laughing, sobbing, he raised his arms in a beckoning embrace. Thus invited, the entity stepped into the room. Two lumbering steps and it loomed over him, its hot breath a glorious tide washing over Noah as he closed his eyes and waited for oblivion.

FOUND FAMILY
JO QUENELL

He placed the pills on the table. They sat silently for some time, staring at the capsules before them. The doomsday clock ticked outside their sterile bedroom, counting final moments.

He smiled at her, teary eyed. She forced herself to do the same.

"How long do you think it will take?"

"Not long," he said. "Salem said they're the same grade given to soldiers in case of capture. Should work before we can feel anything."

Her eyes returned to the pills. His stare remained on her and she worried he could read thoughts.

"Are you scared?"

She shrugged. "You?"

His smile widened. For a moment the dreamy glaze left his eyes and she remembered him as he used to be.

"Remember our bike trip through Yellowstone?"

"I could never forget," she said.

"I never told you how nervous I was the first night we camped. How I had a panic attack once you were asleep. That night I knew you were the braver one between us. I was positive we'd get found by a forest ranger, or someone worse. The cis might get a night in a cell, tops. You know that we'd get worse.

"But then I remember lying on my back and staring at the sky. Just being in fucking awe of the galaxy on display in front of me. All those goddamn stars were unlike anything I've ever seen. You know that cliche about feeling like a speck when staring at space? I get it. Everything we'd gotten used to feeling in the city, all the bullshit we'd never stop complaining about? None of it mattered anymore. And that made me feel safe. It brought me back from an awful place. Nothing had ever felt that way before."

He reached across the table and took her hand. Their touch trembled.

"The closest I've felt since that night has been our time here. And that's coming to an end. But where we're going next? That's past the safety of the stars. It's something new. Something better."

She breathed deep, her exhale rattling. "You're right. I–I know you are. It's just…" her eyes shifted again to the capsules. "These scare me."

He chuckled. "We won't die. We'll transcend. Those are a catalyst, that's all." He squeezed her hand. "I'm more scared of what comes if we stay."

She chewed nervously at her chapped lip. "We don't know if Salem's right. We're gambling with the visions in someone's fever dreams. What if…"

She swallowed. Finally saying the words aloud felt like sacrilege.

"What if this is all bullshit?"

Something changed in his stare, and she knew she'd said too much.

"Okay. Say you're right." His grip on her hand

tightened. "Say we don't go anywhere, and everyone on the outside remembers us as idiots and wingnuts. What will there be to stick around for? Even if Salem's dead wrong, what we have here can't last. If it's not the feds sweeping in, it will be the militias. And I'd rather die here with you, rather than on their terms."

Outside, the doomsday clock stopped ticking. There was no gong, no blast of a horn, no tremors as the world began imploding. Only silence. His face lit up and her heart sank.

"It's time," he said.

They picked their pills off the table. He placed it on his tongue while she paused, unable to drop it in her mouth. An urgent look spread across his face.

"You have to do it now," he said. "It's only a small window to cross over, and–"

"I know," she said, and placed the pill on her tongue.

He smiled, then cupped her face with his hands. Leaned over and kissed her softly, then again with passion. Tears wet her stubbled cheeks as she smelled him, tasted him, for one final time.

He gently pulled away, returning his hands to hers and squeezing tight.

"I love you more than this world and the next," he said, and bit down on his capsule.

She spit hers out on the table.

"I can't," she gasped. "I'm sorry. I just…"

His eyes widened with a look between sadness and betrayal. His face darkened and his body tensed, tightening the cords of his neck. A mess of foam and blood bubbled between his lips and dribbled down his chin. He slipped from his chair to the floor and she watched him seize, the room thickening with the smell of almonds and shit.

Within a minute he lay still.

She stared at him for a while, too shocked to cry, too stunned to move. He still resembled the man she loved, though so much about him was already long dead. She had already eulogized the cute trans boy she'd met working at the coffee shop on Pike street. She had just watched a stranger die.

She finally left her chair and managed to turn her

brain to autopilot. Moving with purpose, she darted to her bed and pulled the sheets away. She tore into the stitched up hole in their mattress and pulled the paring knife free. It would do little damage, but it was all she could take unnoticed from her kitchen shift. Better than nothing if a crisis rose.

She hurried to the sink and found his razor. Wet its blade and shaved the stubble that still grew on her face. Without cisgender eyes scoping her in public, she found herself without a real reason to shave. The miserable hours she had invested into laser and electrolysis in the old world hadn't left her with much more than blonde stubble. But it had grown long enough that it could get her clocked outside of these walls. She'd need to remain unnoticed.

After grabbing her bag from the closet, she hurried out the door and into the bunker's hallway. Everything was so still, so eerie. Every breath was amplified by the surrounding silence. Some of the doors lining the halls were closed, others ajar. She peered into the rooms, at bodies face-down at tables, soaking in puddles of sickness. Others lay naked in their cots. In one room a lifeless parent cradled the stiff body of their young androgynous child. A hand-drawn picture book lay beside them, its pages soaked with foam.

She fought back a sob and forced her eyes to stare straight ahead, down the hallway and into the communal hall. Her knees threatening to give out with each step.

She froze at the entrance to the great room. It seemed impossible to even imagine a scene worse than the one before her. She saw faces of those she'd known as siblings, aunties, friends, occasional lovers. Those who had also been raised around words like *sissy*, *faggot* or *tranny*, those who'd come here tired of the hatred in the world outside. None of them had family so they created something beautiful instead.

Now the stink of senseless death spilled from the mass of them; bodies splayed across the floor, a mass of white gowns and cooling skin. Gripping her paring knife, she started towards the center of the mass. She tried to avoid stepping on the lifeless bodies of her found family. Tried thinking of them as they had been before all of this. When that didn't work, she tried not thinking at all.

Salem lay propped on the corpses of admirers in the center of the room, arms spread like a genderless Christ. For the first time since the fevers and the visions began, there was peace on their face. They had suffered, and she knew that—she wanted more than anything to empathize. But the collateral of their paranoid hallucinations sprawled around her and she resisted digging her knife into Salem's eyes.

Instead she knelt beside them, avoiding their face as she searched. It didn't take long—the key ring sat in the left pocket of their gown. She grabbed the keys and stood, a thrum of victor reverberating through her. She stumbled over the bodies, toward the bunker's entrance.

She was really leaving.

She considered her plan once more while rallying down another hallway, towards the bunker's single door. Get out. Keep going until finding the highway. Hope that whoever picks her up isn't the type who will clock a girl and act in rage. She tried to remember the nearest where the nearest town resembling some safety may be—Missoula, she thought. She tried to remember the names of the lesbian couple they had stayed with on their way up to the bunker—maybe they could provide her a bed while she tried to figure out her next steps.

The sight of the entrance was enough to make her cheer. She removed the key loop from her gown pocket and began trying the dozen or so keys on the heavy door. She clenched her teeth as she fought off the anxiety rising in her chest with every failed attempt. What if, in a state of mania, Salem hid the key, or swallowed it? What if she was trapped with a sea of corpses? The thought chilled her marrow.

It all went away when the tenth key unlocked the door. She couldn't stop the relief from escaping her mouth in a joyous sob. In a few feet she would be free to return to the old world, her old life. Those times before him, before his growing fear of the world pushed them into a separatist bunker. She knew the world out there was a cruel place, but she was willing to accept those imperfections if it meant freedom from the death surrounding her.

Leaving her keys in the lock, she opened the door and started across the threshold.

She froze. Her heart sank.

A thick ethereal fog submerged the old world—a dense, rusty blanket. A putrid stench emanated from the cloud, strong enough to taste. She stumbled back, gagging, covering her mouth.

The fog crept past the doorway and into the bunker, burning her eyes and blistering her skin. She staggered backwards, screaming. A low, wretched moan roiled from the otherside of the doorway, and something long and spindly burst through the fog. It caught her in the stomach, slamming her into the wall behind her.

The growl of the thing escalated into a roar as it pushed its razor sharp appendage into her side.

She screamed, her eyes open but her vision blurred into painful static. No pain of the past registered to the piercing barb tearing her innards. A swell of blood rose up her throat and out of her mouth.

She gripped the paring knife and swung at the appendage. The creature's skin was thick but soft, and the small blade slipped in without much fight. The thing in the doorway screamed and thrashed, digging its barb deeper, severing an intestine. She coughed up blood and something thick and foul while her head filled with static. But she continued stabbing with the paring knife, pushing as far as she could into the meat of the creature. Fluid sprayed from the wound, coating her forearm.

She managed to pull the knife towards her, opening a deep gash. The beast pulled out of her with a loud screech. She met the ground with a sob as the thing retreated, regrouping for its next attack.

The fog continued to pollute the hallway, scraping her lungs like sandpaper every time she breathed. She stood, coughing up a bit of herself, and blindly stumbled towards the door. She pressed one hand against her side, holding her stomach in, while groping for the open door with the other. Something in front of her let out a raspy breath. She anticipated the beast coming back for round two, ready to tear her apart. A much-needed win strengthened her resolve as she grabbed the edge of the heavy door. She put her entire weight into pushing it shut. As it closed, the thing on the other side screamed. Something slammed against the door so hard she could feel it vibrate. She screamed and reinforced it with both hands, hoping to hell it wouldn't push back open.

Her stomach spilled out.

She fell to her knees, screaming between clenched teeth. She tried to push the swelling mass of intestine back inside of herself with one hand, while grasping at the key with the other. She turned the lock as her gore-slicked hand slipped and more of her fell out. She buckled over, sobbing from a mix of triumph, pain, exhaustion, and hopelessness.

Trapped in, once more.

She crawled down the hallway, leaving a trail of herself behind. Back towards the bodies. Back towards her family. Returning to the communal hall felt like a personal feat. The room spun as the pain switched from sharp to dull to sharper. She stopped crawling and lay on the ground, fighting for breath as her vision cleared.

When she looked up, the room was empty.

No bodies. Nothing but discarded white gowns, crumpled where her family lay dead. She resumed her desperate crawl across the floor, the pain numbed by her sheer disbelief. She continued back down the hallway toward her bedroom. Each labored motion felt like her last. She glanced through open doors, into empty barracks.

It couldn't be true.

It *couldn't*.

When she reached her bedroom, he was gone. All that remained was his soiled gown and a puddle of foamy puke. She crawled back toward the table, grappling for her chair. The pain prevented her from standing. She coughed up dark clots and cried in frustration. Then she grabbed the table by the leg and overturned it with the last energy she could muster. The crash echoed through the cold room. She turned her broken body to the tabletop lying next to her. Pawed a bloody hand at the ground around it, looking for what was hers.

"No," she murmured, then screamed. "No!"

She couldn't find her pill. It was gone, just like her family. Vanished through the ether, for all she knew.

All she had left was herself, trapped and dying.

She was cold; colder than she had ever been before. She wanted to crawl over to her thin mattress and bury herself under the sheets until death came. But she couldn't move anymore. Couldn't stop shivering. The puddle forming beneath her was losing its heat and so was she. She began her own escape–no dash into a new world, but instead a slow drift into a long, warm sleep.

She closed her eyes and awaited transcendence.

Jo Quenell lives in Washington State and writes. She is the author of *The Mud Ballad*.

Sam Richard is the author of *Grief Rituals*, *Sabbath of the Fox-Devils*, and the Wonderland Award-Winning Collection *To Wallow in Ash & Other Sorrows*. He is the editor of several anthologies, including the Splatterpunk Award-Nominated *The New Flesh: A Literary Tribute to David Cronenberg*, *Stories of the Eye*, and *Cinema Viscera*. His short fiction litters the landscape of various anthologies and magazines. Widowed in 2017, he slowly rots in Minneapolis. You can stalk him @SammyTotep on twitter.

Justin Lutz is a Splatterpunk Award nominated writer, musician, and screen printer living on the river in Pennsylvania with his wife and cats. He is the Author of the novella *Gemini Rising*, the charity novelette *ACAB Includes Animal Control*, and the short story collection *Gone To Seed*. His short work has appeared in *Teenage Grave*, *Gravely Unusual*, and Ghoulish Tales. As a member of the Void Collective he helps conjure Voidcon and is one of six to collectively summon the *Void Haus*. He believes in Bigfoot, strong coffee, and the healing power of Bruce Springsteen.

Brendan Vidito is the author of the Wonderland Award-winning collection, *Nightmares in Ecstasy* (Clash Books, 2018) and *Pornography for the End of the World* (Weirdpunk Books, 2022). He also co-edited the Splatterpunk Award-nominated anthology *The New Flesh: A Literary Tribute to David Cronenberg* (Weirdpunk Books, 2019) with Sam Richard. He lives in Ontario. You can visit him at brendanvidito.com.

"MISFIT FICTIONS" filthyloot.com
@filthyloot

FILTHY LOOT is an independent press, based out of Ames, IA. Focused on misfit fictions and odd other ideas — we publish books, zines and assorted miscellany in both open and limited edition formats.

- ☐ *a beginner's guide to extreme horror* by Jon Steffens & Ira Rat
- ☐ *Dirt in the Sky* (Anthology)
- ☐ *Fucked Up Stories to Read in the Daytime* (Anthology)
- ☐ *Gone to Seed* by Justin Lutz
- ☐ *Hairs* by Ira Rat
- ☐ *Hollow Coin* by S.T. Cartledge
- ☐ *Isolation is Safety* (Anthology)
- ☐ *LAZERMALL* (Anthology)
- ☐ *My Mind is Not a Billboard//What's Your Favorite TV Show?* by Sam Pink
- ☐ *Pacifier* by Ira Rat
- ☐ *Participation Trophy* by Ira Rat
- ☐ *Shagging the Boss* by Rebecca Rowland
- ☐ *Soft Ceremonies* (Anthology)
- ☐ *TEENAGE GRAVE* 2 (Anthology)
- ☐ *TEENAGE GRAVE* 22 (Anthology)
- ☐ *The Doom that Came To Mellonville* by Madison McSweeny
- ☐ *The God in the Hills and Other Horrors* by Jon Steffens
- ☐ *The God in the Hills 2: Abhorent Flesh* by Jon Steffens
- ☐ *The Vine that Ate the Starlet* by Madeleine Swann
- ☐ *Wax and Wane* by Saoirse Ní Chiaragáin

www.ingramcontent.com/pod-product-compliance
Lightning Source LLC
LaVergne TN
LVHW041616070526
838199LV00052B/3165